NORWOOD HOUSE PRESS

Terrific Transportation

By Kathleen Corrigan

Search for Sounds
Consonants: b, d, j, k, p, q, t, v, z

Scan this code to access the Teacher's Notes for this series or visit
www.norwoodhousepress.com/decodables

DEAR CAREGIVER, *The Decodables* series contains books following a systematic, cumulative phonics scope and sequence aligned with the science of reading. Each book in the *Search for Sounds* series allows its reader to apply their phonemic awareness and phonics knowledge in engaging and relatable texts. The keywords within each text have been carefully selected to allow readers to identify pictures beginning with sounds and letters they have been explicitly taught.

When reading these books with your child, encourage them to isolate the beginning sound in the keywords, find the corresponding picture, and identify the letter that makes the beginning sound by pointing to the letter placed in the corner of each page. Rereading the texts multiple times will allow your child the opportunity to build their letter sound fluency, a skill necessary for decoding.

You can be confident you are providing your child with opportunities to build their foundational decoding abilities which will encourage their independence as they become lifelong readers.

Happy Reading!

Emily Nudds, M.S. Ed Literacy
Literacy Consultant

HOW TO USE THIS BOOK

Read this text with your child as they engage with each page. Then, read each keyword and ask them to isolate the beginning sound before finding the corresponding picture in the illustration. Encourage finding and pointing to the corresponding letter in the corner of the page. Additional reinforcement activities can be found in the Teacher's Notes.

Terrific Transportation
b, t, v

<table>
<tr>
<td>Pages 2 and 3</td>
<td>Hi everyone! My name is Bob. I am five years old. I am one of the boys in my kindergarten class. My class is learning about transportation. Do you know what transportation is? My teacher says it is the way we travel from place to place, or how things are carried from one place to another place. We can walk or run, but usually we use vehicles for transportation.</td>
</tr>
<tr>
<td></td>
<td>My teacher put up a poster that shows some vehicles. The poster gave us an idea. My friends Zara, Victor, and I are hunting for transportation toys in our classroom. It is lots of fun. We have found a van, a jet, a bus, a bulldozer, two trucks, two boats, and a digger.</td>
</tr>
<tr>
<td></td>
<td>Look at Zara jump! She has found another vehicle. It is a bike. Now we have ten vehicles. Can you name them all?</td>
</tr>
</table>

Keywords: bike, blocks, boats, Bob, boys, bus, teacher, toys, van, vehicles, Victor

d, p, t

Pages 4 and 5

Vehicles can be tools for workers. Construction workers use big vehicles to help them build bridges, buildings, and roads. A digger scoops the dirt out of the ground. This one is making a basement for a new building. A bulldozer can push the dirt to make the ground smooth. A dump truck carries important things to the builders and takes junk away.

Some workers travel a lot in their vehicles. A taxi driver drives around taking people where they need to go. A tow truck driver helps vans, cars, and trucks that get stuck. And a police officer needs a good police car to rush to people who need help.

Some workers travel on water for work. Barges are like water trucks. They carry big loads down a river or lake. Tugboats help other boats get where they need to go.

Many other workers, like bus drivers, use vehicles for work. Can you think of some more?

Keywords: digger, dirt, dump truck, people, police car, taxi, tow truck, tugboats

k, p, q

Page 6

Kids and grownups use vehicles when they are playing and having fun.

When the weather is warm, there are many ways to play on vehicles. Zara and I like to ride our bikes near the lake.

We stop to look at the boats on the lake. Victor is in a kayak with his friend, Quinton. We wave to them, but they are so busy paddling that they don't see us. Victor's dad is paddling standing up!

My mother likes to ride her quad bike in the field by the lake. She is having fun with the people on dirt bikes.

Keywords: kayak, kickstand, paddling, people, quad, Quinton

Read this text with your child as they engage with each page. Then, read each keyword and ask them to isolate the beginning sound before finding the corresponding picture in the illustration. Encourage finding and pointing to the corresponding letter in the corner of the page. Additional reinforcement activities can be found in the Teacher's Notes.

t, z	
Page 7	We can play on vehicles when the weather is cold, too. I went to a winter festival with my family, and I saw lots of vehicles.
	Some people had fun sliding down a big hill on their toboggans. They could go very fast.
	Other people used the ice rink. They had to stop sometimes to let the Zamboni clear the ice and make it smooth again. I would like to drive a Zamboni when I am big. It looks like fun, and it is an important job.
	After we had been outside for a while, we bought hot chocolate and donuts from a man in a tent. He had other tasty treats to sell, too.
	Did you notice that these vehicles don't have wheels? Sometimes vehicles can slide on the ground instead of turning wheels. I like to slide on the ice in my boots!

Key Words: tent, toboggans, Zamboni, zigzag

b, j, p	
Pages 8 and 9	My school is a busy place. There are lots of kids and everyone must use transportation to get to school. We also need to get from place to place in the building.
	I walk to school with my big brother, so I don't use a vehicle. My transport is walking. Today I have on my boots because it is wet outside.

Jackie comes to school in a special van. It lowers her wheelchair to the ground so she can go right into the playground.

A lot of people come on buses. The buses line up. A teacher watches to make sure everyone gets off safely. Then they go to the school yard.

Zara just got out of a truck. She grabs her backpack and waves goodbye to her dad. He was her driver today. Sometimes her big brother drives her instead.

Zara and I will go to the kindergarten playground to meet Victor and our other friends. We can play with toys or dig, or just run around until the bell rings. Then we will jump, skip, or run to line up.

Keywords: backpack, Bob, boots, brother, buses, Jackie, jump, people, playground

b, d, j, k, p, q, t, v, z

Pages 10 and 11

We have learned so much about transportation in my kindergarten class. We learned that some kinds of transportation work on land. Other kinds of transportation work in water or in the air. We've learned about moving from place to place using our bodies and using vehicles.

Today, Victor, Zara, and I are painting transportation pictures. We are each painting four of our favorite vehicles. I am painting a land picture. Zara is painting an air picture. Victor is painting a water transportation picture.

When we are done, our teacher will help us write the names of each vehicle. I can write a letter for the first sound I hear and she will help me with the rest. Why don't you look at our pictures and see what vehicles we like the best? Do you have other favorites?

Keywords: balloon, Bob, bulldozer, dirt, drawing, dump truck, jet, jet ski, kayak, pirate ship, poster, quad bike, teacher, tugboat, vehicle, Victor, Zamboni, Zara

Norwood House Press • www.norwoodhousepress.com

367N—082023

Library of Congress Cataloging-in-Publication Data has been filed and is available at catalog.loc.gov

Literacy Consultant: Emily Nudds, M.S.Ed Literacy
Editorial and Production Development and Management: Focus Strategic Communications Inc.
Editors: Christine Gaba, Christi Davis-Martell
Illustration Credit: Mindmax
Covers: Shutterstock, Macrovector

Hardcover ISBN: 978-1-68450-725-2   Paperback ISBN: 978-1-68404-861-8
eBook ISBN: 978-1-68404-920-2